Trollz ™

Five Times the Trouble

adapted by Tisha Hamilton

SCHOLASTIC INC.

New York Toronto London Auckland Sydney
Mexico City New Delhi Hong Kong Buenos Aires

Congratrollations!

You get 50 Trollars to spend on Trollz.com just for buying this book!

After you've read the book go to Trollz.com and type in the code below to collect your 50 Trollars and have a chance to earn 300 more!

n8j97xj09077

ISBN 0-439-82825-2

Published by Scholastic Inc.
SCHOLASTIC and associated logos are trademarks
and/or registered trademarks of Scholastic Inc.

12 11 10 9 8 7 6 5 4 3 2 1   6 7 8 9 10/0

Printed in the U.S.A.
First printing, January 2006

Amethyst finally had her glow. Now she could cast spells like her friends, Topaz, Sapphire, Onyx, and Ruby. The five girls called themselves the BFFL—Best Friends For Life. Today her friends surprised Amethyst by taking her to the Spell Shack at the mall to buy spell beads.

First the spellslady sensed Amethyst's aura.

Then she created
a beautiful spell
bead bracelet.

Amethyst could hardly
wait to cast her first spell.

Outside the store, Amethyst used Ruby's spellphone to send a prank spell to Jasper.

It made him bald, but Jasper didn't mind. He thought his new look was cool.

Back at the mall, the girls heard a crash. Their friend Coal had tripped. He brushed himself off and stood up.

"So he's a little bit of a klutz," Amethyst admitted. "I still think he's cute."

"A guy that kinda cute should at least be kinda cool," Ruby said. "Maybe magic would help."

"I don't think there's magic strong enough to help him," Onyx muttered.

Then Sapphire put her brain in gear. "Maybe we can combine our magic and cast the spell together," she said. "We'll have five times the power."

They joined hands and chanted together.
"Though some may say he's just a fool,
our spell will make this boy cool!"

There was a cracking sound. It felt like an
earthquake! That had never happened
before, when the girls cast spells on their own.

The girls blinked and looked around.
"Coal is cool now," Amethyst sighed.
"A little *too* cool."

They had turned their friend into a
life-size ice sculpture!

It didn't look like this spell was going to wear off!

The BFFL didn't want anyone to see Coal frozen like that before they figured out what to do. So they disguised him as a store mannequin. They even fooled the salestroll.

The trollz headed back to the Spell Shack to ask the spellslady for help, but the Spell Shack was closed!

They banged on the door and shouted, but no one came. Then things got really strange.

Suddenly the door slid open. Nervously, the five girls stepped inside. At the back of the store an old wooden door was glowing.

"That's funny," muttered Ruby. "I don't remember seeing that before."

Ruby raised her hand to knock, but
suddenly the door vanished in a
white mist!
"Ready?" Onyx asked. "Let's go."

The girls bravely headed into
the mysterious fog.

They found themselves in a strange back room where an ancient troll greeted them. "I am Obsidian," she said. "I have been waiting for you."

"How did you know we were coming?" Amethyst wondered. "I know many things," Obsidian told them.

Obsidian explained that they had accidentally used *The Magic of the Five.* That's why their spell had been so powerful. "But will Coal turn back to normal?" Amethyst wanted to know.

"Why, no," Obsidian told her. "He will melt unless you reverse the spell."

The girls were horrified. How would they reverse the spell?

Suddenly a pulsing blue portal lit up in one wall. "Follow me," Obsidian said.

The girls hurried after her.

They found themselves amid the ruins of an ancient troll city. "The evil that destroyed this city was awakened by your spell," Obsidian explained.

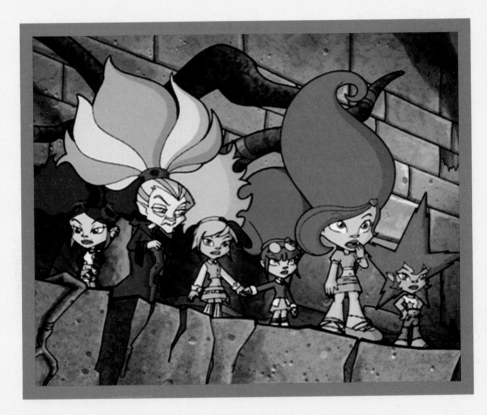

"I can't believe it," Amethyst moaned. "One of my first spells brings on the end of the world!"

Obsidian took them to a grove of oak trees. *"The Magic of the Five* is strongest here," Obsidian went on.

"This is where you must undo your spell by doing it again—in reverse!" She showed them where to put their gems. "Quickly," she urged them.

There was a space for Ruby's star and Onyx's moon. There was a space for Sapphire's flower and Topaz's golden teardrop.

But there wasn't a space for Amethyst's heart anywhere.
"Obsidian, help!" Amethyst called.
No one answered. Obsidian had vanished!

A fierce wind sprang up. Thunder rumbled. The girls heard a spooky growling. A crack opened up in the ground and Amethyst lost her balance.

Her gem flew out of her hands. "My gem!" she wailed.

The gem bounced along the ground. Amethyst tried to grab hold of it, but it kept rolling away. If it fell in the crack, they were doomed!

The gem bounced toward the crack and Amethyst dove for it. There! She had it!

Onyx leaped after her and grabbed her feet.

Then Ruby grabbed onto Onyx. With Sapphire and Topaz helping, they were able to pull Amethyst to safety. Meanwhile the spooky growling grew louder.

"I have an idea," Amethyst said as soon as she was back on solid ground.

Amethyst ran to the oak trees. The other gems were still in place. She realized the other four gems created a space in the center for her heart-shaped one!

Amethyst put her gem there. Suddenly a pink light swirled up into the air.

The girls held hands. "Remember, we have to say the spell backwards this time!" Ruby shouted.

"Cool boy this make will spell our fool a just he's say may some though!" the girls chanted.

The light grew brighter.
Suddenly the girls were back at the mall.

It was as if nothing had happened. Even
their gems were back where they belonged.

The Spell Shack was empty.
Obsidian was nowhere to be found.

"What about Coal?" Amethyst cried.
"I hope he's okay. He was cool to me
even before we cast our spell!"

They raced back to where they'd left him.
Coal was gone. There was only a puddle
of water on the ground.

"He melted!" Amethyst moaned. "What have
we done?"

Then they saw him. He was handing
some wet clothes to the salestroll.
She didn't seem very happy.

When he saw the BFFL,
he grinned. "Whoa,"
he drawled. "Troll babes."

"Coal, are you okay?" Amethyst asked.
"I have no idea," he told her.

All he knew was that he had woken up in a store window. He was still a little surprised.

"Let's go to Fizzy's," Onyx suggested. "I bet you could use a nice cold smoothie, Coal." Fizzy's Amber Caves Café had the best treats in Trollzopolis.

"Uh, sure," Coal answered.
The six of them set out across the mall.

Amethyst smiled shyly at Coal. "Are you sure you're okay?" she asked.
"Well, I think I'll pass on that smoothie," he told her. "But I *would* like a hot chocolate. I'm feeling really chilly."

Amethyst giggled. She was glad she had her friend back!